Moving the Goalposts

D0657650

240

Moving the Goalposts

Rob Childs

Illustrated by Gary Rees

A & C Black · London

GRAFFIX

1 The Listener · Elizabeth Laird
2 Matthew's Goals · Michael Hardcastle
3 Biker · Anthony Masters
4 Captain Hawk · Jim Eldridge
5 Roller Madonnas · Bernard Ashley
6 Otherworld · Jeremy Strong
7 Bodyparts · Theresa Breslin
8 Moving the Goalposts · Rob Childs
9 The Headless Ghost · Pete Johnson
10 Laser Quest · Mick Gowar
11 Roy Kane TV Detective · Steve Bowkett
12 A Boy Like That · Tony Langham
13 Thirteen Candles · Mary Hooper
14 Lovesick · Lynda Waterhouse
15 Hero · Anthony Masters
16 Rapid · Bernard Ashley
17 Hot News · Pete Johnson
18 Goal-getter · Michael Hardcastle
19 The Cinderella Principle · Tony Langham
20 Winners and Losers · Trevor Wadlow
21 The Haunted Surfboard · Anthony Masters
22 Guard Dog · Philip Wooderson

First paperback edition 1998
Reprinted 1999

First published 1998 in hardback by
A & C Black (Publishers) Ltd
35 Bedford Row, London WC1R 4JH

Text copyright © 1998 Rob Childs
Illustrations copyright © 1998 Gary Rees
Cover illustration copyright © 1998 Bob Harvey

The right of Rob Childs to be identified as author of this work has been asserted by him in accordance with the Copyrights, Designs and Patents Act 1988.

ISBN 0-7136-4903-8

A CIP catalogue record for this book is available from the British Library.

All rights reserved. No part of this publication may be reproduced in any form or by any means - graphic, electronic or mechanical, including photocopying, recording, taping or information storage and retrieval systems - without the prior permission in writing of the publishers.

Printed in Great Britain by William Clowes Ltd,
Beccles, Suffolk.

Penalty!

Sam crouched on the goal-line, feeling as if the whole world was watching him. He fidgeted with his gloves, knocking the mud off them, and bounced up and down on his toes.

He glanced around at his team-mates. They were strung along the edge of the penalty area like a row of blue shirts on a washing line.

Sam knew the score all right. They didn't have to tell him that. But Daniel, the team captain, wanted Sam to be aware of something else.

The penalty-taker smiled. He decided to play a game of double-bluff, hoping the keeper would think he'd aim to the right.

On the referee's whistle, the boy loped forwards and did a little jink run-up to try and confuse the keeper even more. His body disguised the direction of the kick well, but Sam saw the flicker of the eyes that gave him away.

As he struck the ball to the left, Sam dived.
Great stop!
Magic, Sam! Saved us again.
SMACK
Sam scrambled to his feet, grinning hugely and hugging the ball to his chest. Southfield School's Year 7 soccer team mobbed their goalie in delight.
C'mon, team. Sam's kept us in the game. Let's grab that equaliser now.

Sam booted the ball away upfield, but it soon came back into his own half. The home team were proving too strong. They had dominated the match right from their first attack.

On the touchline, Southfield's sports teacher, Mr Rogers, shook his head.

But even Sam couldn't prevent a second goal for ever. Ten minutes from the end, a tall striker leapt, unchallenged, for a corner and headed the ball firmly past the helpless keeper.

Reckon it had to come some time. They're playing us off the park.
No wonder they're top of the league.
Keep your heads up. It's not over yet, keep battling.
Ajit, Southfield's leading scorer, was not impressed by the teacher's demands.
Huh! OK for him to say that. He's not out here getting stuffed. I've been tripped and kicked all match and their ref hasn't given us a single foul.

There was no further scoring until the final minute of the game. The goal went to Southfield, but it only proved a consolation effort. A rare lapse by his marker allowed Ajit a clear view of the target and he tucked his shot neatly into the net.

It was soon to become much worse for Sam. As they changed in the cloakroom, Mr Rogers called out above the noise.

It was an honour they all dreaded. His team-mates cheered with relief that the teacher hadn't picked on them this time. Mr Rogers seemed to enjoy watching someone squirm in front of a smirking Year Group assembly, especially if the player had to explain how a match was lost.

Sam didn't hear the comments. His senses had been numbed. Leering faces swam before his eyes, the sound distorted. All the pleasure and excitement of his performance had suddenly vanished. A sense of panic washed over him instead and sweat broke out on his forehead.

In desperation, still half-dressed, he went up to the teacher to try and have a word in private.

Sam hoped nobody could overhear what he said, but the teacher's reply was agonisingly loud.

Sam glanced round nervously, knowing that his team-mates were listening.

Sam shuffled his bare feet.

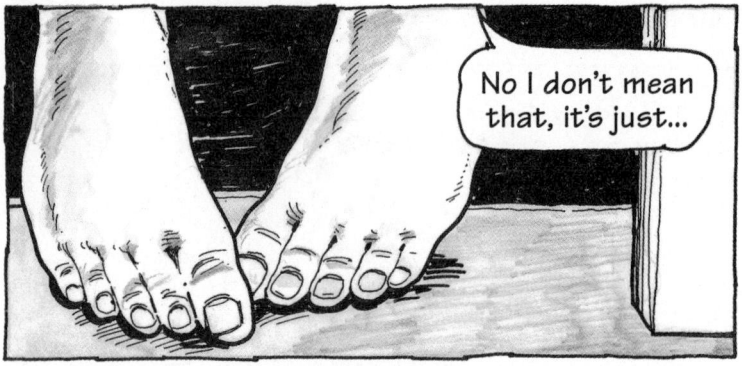

'No excuses,' said the teacher, losing his patience.

Sam was the last one to leave the changing room, unable to find his socks. He was past caring. He stuck his feet into his cold trainers and slouched into the car park.

Daniel's parents were waiting to drive him home. He climbed into the car without speaking, his face sickly white.

Come on, it won't be that bad. Best to try and make it funny so we can all have a good laugh.
You'll all have a good laugh OK - at me.
Don't be daft. Remember Ajit making jokes about how useless we all were? He said your handling was so bad, you couldn't even catch a bus!
Well, now's your chance to get your own back on him.

Sam smiled weakly, trying to hide his fears. He hadn't told his mates the real reason why he'd got on the wrong bus that day after the match.

The truth was that he'd read the number back to front, mistaking 12 for 21.

For Sam didn't always see things quite like other people. He tended to jumble up numbers, and his letters too, without realising. Until recently, he hadn't understood why his reading and spelling were so poor, but now he knew.

After he'd attempted a series of tests, an educational psychologist had explained to his parents what was different about him. He was dyslexic.

Out of Action

Sam was away from school until Thursday. On his return, he was greeted in the classroom by Ajit who seemed to delight in telling him the bad news.

I can't help being sick.
What, sick of school?
Sam shrugged and gave him a quick grin.
Yeah, well, something like that. I'll just have to keep out of his way for a bit, I guess.

Mrs Brown, their form teacher, came into the room.
Pleased to see you back, Sam - and I know somebody else who will be as well.
Who's that, Miss?
Mr Rogers. He wants you to go to the changing rooms straight after registration. I'm not sure what it's about.
A few sniggers were heard around the room. Everyone else knew.

Daniel and Josh, the team's centre-back, caught up with a miserable-looking Sam at morning break.

The captain was horrified.
But we need you. Nobody else is any good in goal.
Dad will go beserk when he hears. He knows what was making me ill.
The thought of having to write that report, you mean?
Sam nodded.
He's already planning to come in and have a word with Mrs Brown about things.

Sam felt his fists clench. Josh often came out with snide remarks when he saw Sam struggling to do something in class.

Sam moved menacingly towards Josh, making him back-pedal.
Disconnected am I? Right - maybe I'll disconnect you now, bit by bit! See how you like it.
Josh quickly made himself scarce.
Ignore him, Sam, you know what he's like. Let's go and join in the kickabout on the field.

Sam's mood improved when he felt a football in his hands again.
He took his frustration out on the ball by hoofing it powerfully away at any opportunity.
First he pretended it was Josh's head, then Mr Rogers', and by the bell he felt more like his old self again.

By Saturday morning, though, Sam still hadn't got over the disappointment of having to miss the match. He turned up to watch instead and could hardly believe his eyes. Their wooden goalposts were lying on the pitch, broken into pieces. The footballers stared at the wreckage in dismay.

I bet it's that same gang who smashed up those other posts a while back.
Rogers said if it happened once more, that'd be it. The school can't afford to keep replacing them.
Ajit pointed to a set of bigger goals on another pitch.
We'll just have to use them instead.

They're huge. The older lads play in them, not us.
I don't mind. It'll give me more chance to score!
Sam pulled a face at him
OK for you, maybe. Not for us poor keepers. I can't even touch the crossbar on those goals.

Neither could the reserve goalkeeper. The very first shot of the game soared over his head out of reach - but still passed underneath the high bar into the goal. So did another soon afterwards. The reserve's confidence was shattered and he even ended up letting two goals in through his legs.

How Sam wished he could have been playing. The team might still have lost, but perhaps not so heavily. The final score was 8-2 and Sam felt he had somehow let everyone down.

The team's next soccer practice on Tuesday afternoon took place in the big goals too. Ajit loved it. Within minutes he chipped the ball into the far top corner, well beyond Sam's flailing arms.

Sam hated letting in goals at the best of times. He couldn't bear the thought of being beaten by unstoppable shots in all their future home games. When he complained, Mr Rogers merely responded with a shrug.

Sam sat in the classroom with them, but he was only half listening to the conversation. It seemed that there wasn't enough money to pay for a specialist teacher to give him the extra help that he needed to cope with his work.

We're all trying to do our best for Sam, but I'm afraid our hands are tied. The Education Authority keeps moving the goalposts.
Sam's interest suddenly perked up when he heard that.
Moving the goalposts? What does that mean, Miss?

His teacher attempted to explain.
It means that the Authority keeps coming up with different reasons - or excuses - why they can't provide the funding to employ somebody to work with you for a few hours each week.

As his dad continued to discuss the situation with Mrs Brown, Sam turned the new phrase over in his mind.

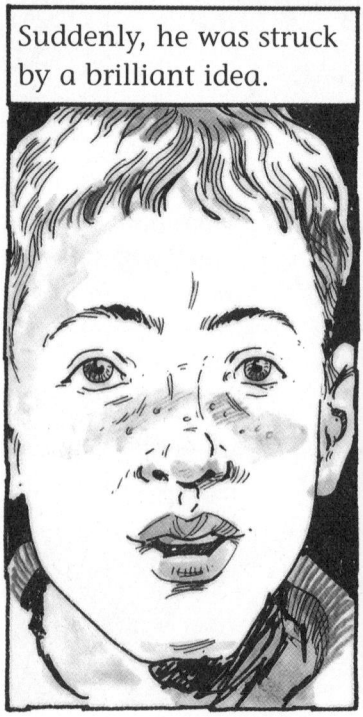

Designer Goals

Sam was busy that evening. The dining table was covered with paper and the waste bin by his chair was full of crumpled sheets.

Funny looking goals. They're all in pieces.
Exactly. They're movable! The idea came to me this afternoon.
His dad studied Sam's unfinished designs with increasing interest.
Excellent, Sam, I can try and get some cheap metal tubing from the factory. I could give you a hand at the weekend if you like?
Thanks, Dad.

Sam wanted to check that the spelling was correct before he showed the plans to Mr Rogers. Mum helped him with that.

The only words he was sure about were those of his own name. He'd learnt them off by heart years ago, but he didn't always notice if his 'N's and 'S's were the right way round. He scrawled the title across the top in capital letters.

Sam worked with his dad all weekend, measuring, cutting and drilling the long tubes of metal. They welded some of the sections together, but others were fixed by bolts so that they could be taken apart.

At Sunday teatime, Sam gave Mum a progress report.

Sam made a point of speaking to the sports teacher first thing on Monday morning.
Me and my dad are making these vandal-proof, metal goals for the school, Mr Rogers.
Great. How big are they?

They can be as big as the ones we still have - and as small as the ones that were smashed.
I don't understand.
Hmm...perhaps we can try them out in the game on Saturday, if they're ready in time.
Well, the posts and crossbar can all be made longer or shorter. You know, like a sliding telescope!
Er, why are you doing all this?
Because I don't want to have to play in those massive goals again till I'm older - and taller!

Sam returned to the team on Wednesday for a friendly fixture that they won 4-1, thanks to a hat-trick from Ajit. But as they changed happily afterwards, the boys knew that Saturday's cup-tie against Brimthorpe would be much tougher.

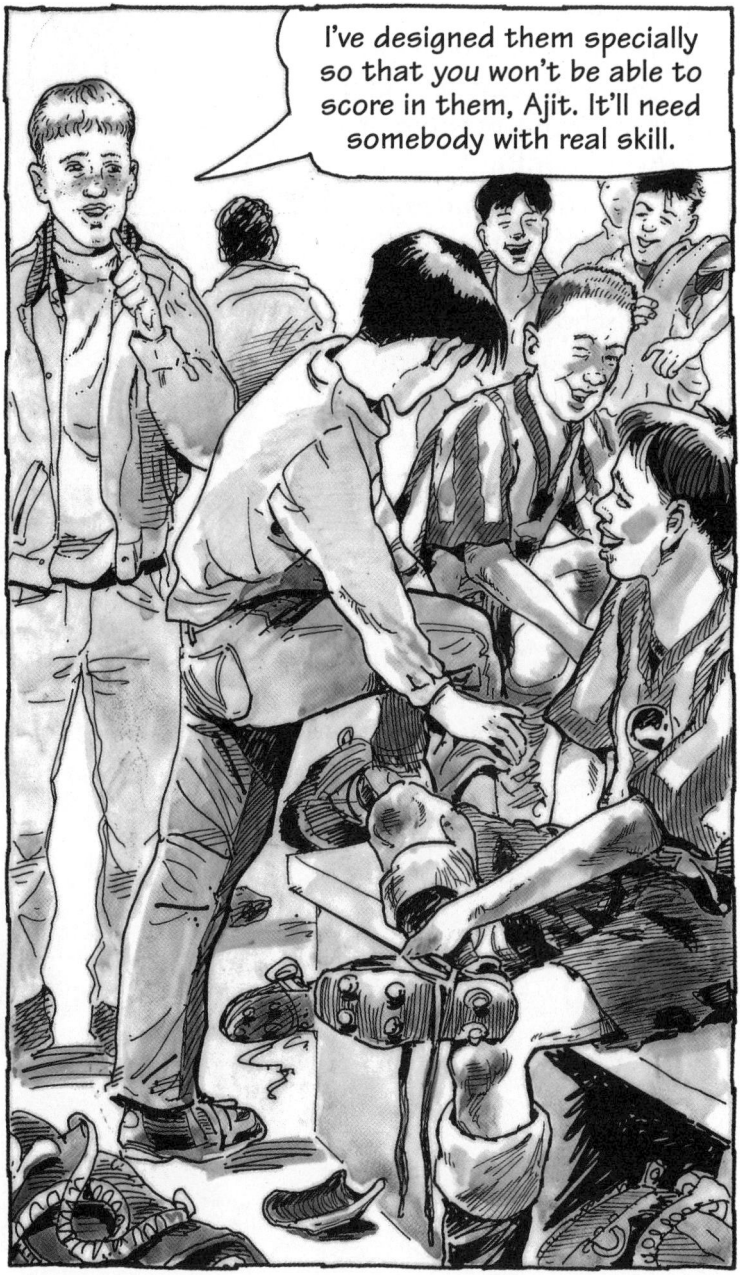
I've designed them specially so that you won't be able to score in them, Ajit. It'll need somebody with real skill.

The goals *were* ready in time - but only just. Sam spent Friday evening giving them their final coat of white paint, his head still reeling from the exciting news he'd heard that day. The school had at last received an extra grant of money to use for the benefit of all their dyslexic pupils.
About time, too. The individual teaching will be a tremendous help in improving your reading and writing abilities, Sam. And I'm sure you'll make the most of it.

EASTER CARMUIRS PRIMARY SCHOOL

They're magic, Sam. Much better than using those big 'uns.
Yeah, best own goal I've ever seen!
Huh! Not even any nets on them.
Sam heard Josh's loud sneer but let the remark pass. None of the school's goals had nets either.

I'm going in to get changed now, Dad.
Sam stopped dead in his tracks.
Oh, no! I've forgotten my kit. I've gone and left all my goalie gear at home.
Your memory's worse than mine. You'll just have to see what you can borrow.

Ten minutes later, Sam trooped out of the changing room feeling strange and nervous. Strange because of his baggy top, odd socks and tight boots. Nervous because he so much wanted his goals to be a success.

At least Mr Rogers had told him they seemed fine, even though the teacher hadn't had the chance to inspect them close-up yet.

It didn't take long for the new goals to be christened.

Unfortunately, the dubious honour of being the first keeper to concede a goal in them fell to their maker. Sam lay on the wet ground, well beaten by a deflected, skidding drive.

As Sam picked himself up, he was in for a surprise. Josh actually apologized.
Bit cruel, that deflection! Soz! I tried to block the shot.
Not your fault. Just forget it and get on with the game.

With the wind in their favour, Southfield hit back strongly and forced Brimthorpe on to the defensive.

The glistening posts soon sported their first dirty mark as a volley from Ajit clanged against one of the metal uprights.

A swift counter-attack from the visitors, however, almost put Southfield further behind.

Always on the alert, Sam dived full-length to pull off an acrobatic save, turning the ball around a post for a corner.

This swung across into the goalmouth and a furious scramble was ended only by the ball being blasted just over the crossbar.

That comment from Josh was music to Sam's ears. It made every minute spent working on the goals seem worthwhile.

It was the captain himself who finally levelled the scores.

Same for both sides?

Brimthorpe's penalty area was under almost constant siege for the remainder of the first half. Sam had little to do and he became aware of people on the touchline pointing at one goal and then the other.

The Brimthorpe teacher called out to Mr Rogers.
Hey, ref! Stop the game!
It's not half-time yet. What's the matter?
The man strode over to the Brimthorpe goal and paced out the distance between the posts.

Sam's heart sank when he saw him start to head up the pitch in his direction.
What are you doing?
I reckon our goal is bigger than yours - and I'm going to prove it.
It can't be, surely. They are adjustable, but...

Hey! Nice one, Sam. Wish I'd thought of a trick like this.
Was your dad going to sneak up and alter them at half-time, so ours was still smaller when we changed ends?
Don't be stupid. It wasn't done on purpose.
SOUTHFIELD

Sam tried to explain to the teachers as well.

Sam's pitiful face was enough to convince anyone he was telling the truth.

His dad rushed on to the scene, breathless and embarrassed after finding out what had happened.

Sam spoke up again.
Dad and me will sort out the goals so they're both the same size.
It was a genuine offer from Sam, but it made the Brimthorpe teacher laugh out loud.
No way! You'll leave them exactly as they are now. We'll see how you get on guarding a bigger goal for the rest of the match.

Sam came in for some mickey-taking from his team-mates at half-time, but he took it in the right spirit.
Yeah, we must do it again another time.
Worth a try, Sam, it nearly worked!
Anybody can make a mistake. It's just that I seem to make them more than most.

Daniel summed up the battle that lay ahead.
None of us can afford to make any mistakes this half. They're really gonna throw everything at us, knowing our goal is bigger.
Same for both sides in the end, though, I suppose.
Not in this weather, it isn't. It's blowing a gale now - and it's starting to rain.

The captain turned to his goalkeeper.
You've got to be on top form, Sam. We're relying on you.
Yeah. You got us into this mess, so you can get us out of it!

As the second-half kicked off, the wind and rain lashed into the faces of the Southfield players. Sam swallowed hard, grateful that at least he'd be able to grip the wet ball better now that he had his gloves.

Sam was called into action straight away as a shot curled and dipped in the swirling wind. Somehow, he managed to get his hands and body behind the ball, dropping to his knees and clinging safely on to it.

The busier he became, the better he played. He made a whole string of good saves, including touching a powerful, close-range header on to the crossbar.

Nobody could quite believe it when Southfield broke away and snatched the lead, totally against the run of play.

As time began to run out for the visitors, they became more and more frantic. Their shooting was often wild, too high or wide, even with the bigger goal to aim at.

Sam dealt well with anything they managed to get on target...

'Goal, ref!' claimed the Brimthorpe captain loudly. 'It went just inside the post. Anybody could see that.'

To Southfield's astonishment, instead of giving a corner, Mr Rogers suddenly pointed to the centre-circle.

I couldn't be absolutely sure from my angle. Felt I had to give them the benefit of the doubt after all that business earlier.

Boosted by the gift of an equaliser, Brimthorpe nearly went and scored the winner. In a last mad scramble in Sam's muddy penalty area, he blocked one effort from point-blank range and then Josh kicked another off the line.
The two boys grinned at each other.
Thanks for that one, Josh.

Any time, Sam. You've played a blinder. No hard feelings, I hope, pal?
No, just be behind me like that in future when I need you!

The final whistle signalled a 2-2 draw and the boys were confident they could win the replay. To no-one's great surprise, Mr Rogers again named Sam as 'Man of the Match', but this time he made sure he put Sam's mind at rest first.

Sam smiled sheepishly.
Not yet, thanks, Mr Rogers. Maybe when I've got a bit better at that sort of thing.
His dad was waiting for him outside and gave him a slap on the back.
Well played, son. You showed 'em what you can do.

Dad slipped Sam a wink.

And I reckon you'll be able to start achieving your potential in the classroom now, too.
Right! The only goalposts that are going to keep moving are these on the soccer pitch!